GRAND SLAM

EVAN JACOBS

SADDLEBACK
EDUCATIONAL PUBLISHING

WH/TE L/GHTNING
BOOKS

BEHIND THE MASK	IGGY	SCRATCH N' SNITCH
BREAK AND ENTER	ON THE RUN	SUMMER CAMP
EMOJI OF DOOM	QWIK CUTTER	THE UNDERDOGS
GRAND SLAM	REBEL	UNDER THE STAIRS

SADDLEBACK
EDUCATIONAL PUBLISHING
www.sdlback.com

ISBN-13: 978-1-68021-107-8
ISBN-10: 1-68021-107-2
eBook: 978-1-63078-424-9

Printed in Malaysia

21 20 19 18 17   1 2 3 4 5

ABOUT THE GAME OF TENNIS

DEFINITION OF GRAND SLAM WINNING ALL 4 MAJORS AT ANY POINT DURING THE COURSE OF A TENNIS CAREER

HENRY VIII HAD MANY TENNIS COURTS BUILT AROUND ENGLAND

24 TONS OF STRAWBERRIES ARE ORDERED EACH YEAR FOR THE CHAMPIONSHIP AT WIMBLEDON

THE STRINGS OF THE TENNIS RACKET WERE MADE OF AND GUTS IN THE PAST

I WILL NEVER LOOK AT PESTO THE SAME WAY!

PRIMO'S PESTO

CHAPTER 1

MATCH POINT

Brad Kingsley wiped the sweat from his brow. He watched his opponent. The boy spun his tennis racket around in his hand. Then he hit the ball against the ground a few times.

"Oh, come on! Don't stall!" Brad whispered. He didn't want anyone to hear him. Brad didn't speak to people like that.

His muscles tensed. Brad hated this part of the game. He knew his opponent was trying to mess with him.

The score was 20–40. His opponent had to score one more point. Brad would lose the match.

Brad had started off well. He'd scored the first two points. Then his mind drifted. He started thinking about other things. Could his opponent sense this? Brad wondered if that was why he was losing now.

Why do I keep playing this game? I can't even focus on it, he thought.

Brad was a sophomore at Valley High School. He had been playing tennis since he was ten. Brad was sixteen now. Varsity tennis was competitive. He was really good.

You play tennis because you're good at it, he told himself. He was trying to pump himself up. It was a trick Coach Kennedy had taught. She was the varsity coach.

Brad was tall and in shape. He had an athletic build. His hair was blond. Brad's green eyes were light.

His biggest challenge was concentration. Brad found it hard. His parents told him he had an auditory processing disorder. Something about his ears and brain not being in sync. He didn't know what that meant. But sometimes he lost his train of thought. It happened a lot when people talked to him. If they didn't say too much, Brad was okay. But sometimes Brad would get confused.

When that happened, he had a few tricks. He would either nod his head, or say nothing. The other person didn't realize they had lost him. He had another trick too. Brad repeated the last thing said to him. He could process the words better this way.

He was a good student. He had math, English, history, biology, and PE. PE was tennis practice. His elective was a resource class. It was not his elective by choice.

Resource was like study hall. Brad's teacher was Mr. Cohen. He was tall. The teacher had a loud voice. But with Brad, Mr. Cohen spoke softly.

Mr. Cohen was from New York. He had an accent. Brad liked it. He liked asking the teacher questions about New York. They chatted when Brad's work was done. The teacher or an aide often helped Brad with his work. After resource class, most of his assignments were done.

Brad didn't like what kids called the resource room. They said it was the "dumb class." Aside from the cruel words, being in resource was fine.

Brad's mind was not on his game.

What should I do later?

Ugh. He was doing it again. His concentration was drifting.

He stared at his opponent. Brad looked at the crowd. There weren't many people. But there were enough for Brad.

He started to think about the heat. His homework. Then he saw his parents. They were sitting in the crowd. Were they looking at him?

His mom was smiling. His dad was serious. Like he wanted to say "Stay focused, Brad!"

People always said that to him. Sometimes it bugged him. Staying focused was often out of his control.

He also saw some kids he didn't know well. He'd noticed them at school.

Brad's eyes focused on a girl. She had long black hair. Her skin was a light olive color. She had dark brown eyes.

The girl smiled at him. The smile seemed to say "I believe in you."

Brad couldn't stop looking at her.

That's when he heard a popping sound.

CHAPTER 2

SERVE

The ball came toward him.

No! Crud. I got distracted.

"Darn it! " Brad said under his breath.

He could hear people gasp.

Brad moved toward the ball. It was headed mid-court. If he missed, the game would be over. He could take the loss. But he didn't want to lose because of his disability.

Brad moved fast. He lifted his racket.

Just lob it over the net!

The ball was coming too fast. He leaped toward it.

Too slow! The ball passed him. He felt the whoosh as his racket hit air.

His teammates groaned.

Brad hit the ground. It didn't hurt. But he was stung with embarrassment.

His opponent cheered. So did the rival tennis team's fans.

Brad stood up. He walked to Coach Kennedy. She was tall, like Mr. Cohen. Coach had short hair. She had played college tennis. That made her a great coach. She always had something positive to say.

"Hey," his opponent called.

Brad looked over. He squeezed his racket.

"Good game, dude."

"Thank you," Brad said. "Congratulations." He didn't smile.

He turned and looked at his coach.

"You played great." She smiled. "The season just started. It's no big deal."

Brad shook his head.

The next players were already on the court. Brad got himself some water. He sat down next to Julian Rodriguez. Julian was Brad's best friend on the team. He talked to Brad the most. Brad thought he was nice.

Everybody else hung out with Scott Nguyen. He was the best player on the team. Scott always made people laugh. He could talk to the girls. They flocked to him.

"Man." Scott shook his head. His voice was low. But loud enough so Brad could hear. "He totally blew that play."

Brad looked over at Scott. Scott and Warren Williams were looking at him. Then they turned their attention to the next game.

Warren was just like Scott.

Those two dudes are good at everything.

"Come on, Cody!" Scott yelled. Other players cheered on their teammate too.

Brad watched the game. He wasn't really watching it, though. He kept thinking about how he'd messed up.

"You tried so hard out there," his father said. They were driving home from the match.

Brad was sitting in the backseat. He rested his head against the seat. His tennis bag was in the trunk.

He was close to his parents. Their relationship was open. They talked about emotions. And he didn't feel weird sharing his feelings. His parents were positive people. Brad was a good kid. They only got on him when he didn't do his chores.

"The way you dove for that last shot," his mom said. "I felt like I was watching a match on TV."

"I lost my focus," Brad said.

"Well, that happens," his mom said. "I lose my focus a lot. Especially when I'm doing something hard."

"Yeah." His dad smiled. "It was a tough match."

His parents continued to talk. Brad looked out the car window. He tuned them out. Not because he didn't want to hear them. He wanted to think.

Who was that girl at the match? The one who had smiled at him. That smile had made him feel good. Brad liked that.

I just want to see her again.

Brad kept looking out the window. He hoped he would see the girl again.

CHAPTER 3

VOLLEY

Do you want to go to the store with me?" Brad's mom asked.

He was sitting in his bedroom. The house was a one-story ranch. His room was bare. He had his bed and desk. The rest of his stuff was in his closet. Clothes. Shoes. Books. DVDs.

"Sure. I just have a few more math problems," he said.

"Okay. Let's go when you're done."

Brad was happy. Most of his homework was done. He'd finished it in his resource class.

The English class was reading *One Flew Over the Cuckoo's Nest.* He had finished reading the assigned chapter. His only other assignments were world history and pre-algebra. He had finished world history. But he still had math homework.

He always did math last. It was his worst subject. Math was just plain hard.

Mr. Rey was the teacher. He'd told Brad help was on the way. Brad didn't like that.

"Help means an aide," he'd told his parents. "I'm going to look stupid. Everyone will know why the aide is there."

But his teacher told him not to worry. Brad would have an aide during math to work with him. Other kids could ask for the aide's help too. But the administration hadn't found one yet.

Yeah, he thought. *Who would choose to be a math aide as their elective?*

It bothered him a lot. He was a sophomore. But he was only learning pre-algebra. It sucked. One sophomore he knew was in calculus.

It took twenty minutes to finish three problems. Then Brad was ready to go to the store.

"I just can't stay focused," Brad said. He was pushing a shopping cart. It was filled with groceries.

"You can," his mom said. She patted his shoulder. "You've won a lot of matches."

"Those guys weren't good."

"Not that good? They're varsity players."

"Why am I even on the team? Aside from Julian, I don't have any friends."

Brad picked up a box of Cheerios. He put it in the cart. "We need these."

"You're a very good tennis player. That's why you're on the team." His mom grabbed some oatmeal. "Your father and I want you to have friends. You're only sophomore."

"Tennis is the only thing I'm really good at. I'm in easy classes. But they're still hard for me."

"Just math." His mom put a loaf of bread into the cart. "You do well in other subjects."

"I'm in pre-algebra, Mom. I'm a sophomore. Maybe I'll get to geometry. Maybe not."

"And that's fine."

"But it's not fine. I need to be better in school. In the real world nobody's going to be nice like you. If I lose my concentration on the job, I'll get fired."

"You'll be fine. You always try your best."

"My best just isn't that good." Brad's voice was low. "I want more friends. I want to be better at school. I'm just not good at it."

"Brad." His mom slowed down. "Just stop. You are being too hard on yourself. All of this will work out. You're only sixteen."

Brad stared at her. He was sad. But he didn't feel like crying. He rarely did.

The two continued shopping. They didn't talk much. Eventually, they got in line.

"Hey," his mom said. "We need pesto sauce. I'll be right back."

"I'll get it," Brad said.

He moved quickly down the aisles. Eventually, he found the pasta section. There was the pesto.

Then his jaw dropped. There she was! The girl from the game was standing there. She was facing the sauces.

It was fate. She was meant to be there.

The girl turned. She saw Brad staring at her.

"Hi," she said, smiling.

"Hey." Brad tried to smile. He felt self-conscious. His smile was lame. Brad tried not to show too many teeth. "Excuse me." He reached in front of her.

"Good game."

Brad stared at her.

She's making fun of me. She watched me blow it. That last serve killed me.

"You really gave that guy a good game."

"Thanks." Maybe she wasn't kidding.

Brad stared into her dark eyes. Her face was perfect. The harsh store lights beamed down. Still, her skin was flawless.

Say something! he told himself.

"Do you watch a lot of tennis?" Lame! But better than just staring at her.

"I've watched some games. Mostly on TV."

"Oh …"

"I am Reese," she said. "Reese Caballero."

"My name's Brad. Brad Kingsley."

They stared at each other.

"I just started at Valley a few weeks ago. I used to go to Bay View," she said.

"Did you want to go to Valley?" Her answer was important to him. But he didn't know why.

"Not particularly. I liked Bay View a lot. My parents bought a house here. It could've been worse, I guess. I already knew so many people at Valley. That made it easier."

Brad shook his head. He didn't have much

experience with chitchat. It was hard talking to Reese. She was so pretty. He couldn't think of what to say next.

A woman appeared. She looked like an older version of Reese.

"Hi, Mom," Reese said. "This is Brad. He plays tennis for Valley."

"Hi, Brad. Nice to meet you."

"Hi," he said. "I'd better go. My mom's in the checkout line."

"Okay. See you at school." Reese smiled at him again.

Wow. Each smile made him feel special.

"Yeah, see you," he said.

As he walked away, he heard Reese's voice. "Mom, he's so cute!" she said.

Brad wanted to turn around. But he didn't. He grinned. Was he cute? He wasn't sure. At least he wasn't ugly. He never paid much attention to how he looked.

He walked over to his mom. The cashier was ringing up her last item. Brad put the pesto jar down by the scanner.

"Did you get lost?" his mom teased. "I wondered what happened to you."

"No. I just couldn't find the pesto." He didn't tell his mom about Reese. He wanted to keep the meeting to himself.

Reese makes me want to do something great.

Brad knew Reese was special. He'd never felt like this before.

CHAPTER 4

BASELINE

Dude, shut up," Dominic said. "Give me more chips."

Brad was sitting at his desk. He was next to Edgar and John. They all had earbuds in their ears. They always listened to music when they worked. There were only ten students in the resource class. It was third period.

Brad couldn't listen to music when he worked. He couldn't watch TV either.

Dominic, Edgar, and John were loud. Mr.

Cohen always yelled at them. The three liked Brad. He didn't know why.

"Mr. Cohen," Brad said. He raised his hand. "I got my *Cuckoo's Nest* questions done."

Mr. Cohen smiled. He walked over to Brad. The teacher was always on his feet. He worked with a different student every few minutes. Brad couldn't figure out how he juggled so many tasks at once.

"This looks great, Brad." Mr. Cohen nodded. "Do you have your math homework done?"

"Yes. I'm working on world history next."

"Sounds good."

Mr. Cohen patted Brad on the shoulder.

"I wish your dedication would rub off on your friends." Mr. Cohen smiled. He nodded toward Dominic and the others.

"Why you gotta diss us, Cohen?" Edgar smiled.

"Yeah," John said. "It's not cool to play favorites."

"It might mess us up in the head." Dominic grinned. "Especially if we think you like Brad more."

"You're already messed up in the head." Mr. Cohen winked. "And I'm not playing favorites. It's a fact. You want to see a good student? Well, look at Brad. You want to see—well, I don't know what to call you three."

"That's cold," Dominic said.

Mr. Cohen walked over to help some seniors on the computer. The seniors were trying to graduate. Their academic program was called Socrates. It was a lot of work. If the students completed it, they would graduate on time.

"Cohen's right." Bernadette smiled. She was another student in resource. "Brad is the best in this class."

"The best looking, you mean." It was Kathryn. She was Bernadette's bestie. And also another resource student.

Brad didn't look at the girls. He took out his

world history. Life was easier if people thought he wasn't paying attention.

Bernadette and Kathryn were chatty. They talked with Brad in class too. The girls hung around Dominic, Edgar, and John. Brad overheard them talking a lot. Sometimes they hooked up. But mostly they were just friends.

"That's not what you said the other night," Dominic said.

"Dominic!" Mr. Cohen wasn't even looking at him. "I don't see you working. I hear talking. Talking is not going to help you pass your classes."

"I didn't say nothin', Cohen!"

"That's because I stopped you. Stop talking. Start working," Mr. Cohen said. "You know the material. I'll be over in a minute to help."

Brad looked at his history assignment. Vocabulary. He liked work like this. "This homework is easy," he'd tell his parents. "I just have to look it up."

The students continued gabbing. Eventually,

the bell rang. They hadn't done much work. Brad was almost all done with his.

the bell rang. They hadn't done much work. Brad was almost all done with his.

Mr. Rey was sitting at his desk. There was a stack of papers. He was grading tests.

The class was working on factoring.

Factoring. Ugh. I hate this stuff.

Brad just didn't get math. Basic arithmetic, yes. Anything beyond basic confused him.

There were thirty problems. The class had been working for ten minutes. Brad had only done two problems. Were they correct? He wasn't sure.

The classroom door opened. There was Reese. What was she doing here? She had her backpack slung over her shoulder. She smiled at Mr. Rey. They started talking.

Maybe she was in pre-algebra too.

Brad felt good. It was meant to be.

"Okay, great," Mr. Rey said. He picked up a stack of papers. Mr. Rey put them on a table next to his desk. "How are your math skills?"

"Pretty good," Reese said. She sat down. Reese started looking at the tests. Mr. Rey gave her what looked like the answer key.

Brad's heart sank.

She's the teacher's aide. I knew she'd be way smarter than me.

He looked back at his work.

Still stuck on the third problem. Man, I'm a loser.

Then he remembered something. His parents always said it. "If you need help, ask for it," they'd say. "You have to advocate for yourself."

But in front of Reese? No way. He didn't want her to think he was dumb. So he picked up his paper. Then went over to Mr. Rey's desk.

"Hi, Brad," Mr. Rey said warmly. Brad was thankful to have a nice teacher in his worst subject.

"I need some help."

"Perfect." Mr. Rey smiled. "This is Reese. She's our new TA. Why don't you two work in the back?"

Brad froze. He thought Reese was hot. Could he concentrate around her?

The two looked at each other. Reese smiled. She stood up and walked to the back. Brad followed her. He looked around. Nobody paid any attention to them.

"So," she said quietly. "We meet again."

"Yeah," Brad said.

"What do you need help with?"

He couldn't speak. She was too beautiful. Her eyes seemed to be controlling him.

"Factoring," he said finally. He handed her his paper. "The third one."

"Ah," Reese said. "Factoring is basically taking a number apart. And showing how the number gets made. Does that make sense?"

"Yeah, sort of."

"Well, take fifty-five. Just looking at that number. What other numbers make it up?"

Brad looked at the number. "Five?"

"Yes." Reese gave him a bright smile. "So, what number could you multiply five by to get close to fifty-five?"

"Ten." For Brad that answer made sense. "That's fifty."

"Exactly. Then how much more do you need to make fifty-five?" Reese eyed Brad. She seemed to be cheering for him. Just like at the tennis match.

"Five."

"Yes! How many fives is that if you already have ten?"

Brad thought for a second. "Eleven."

"You got it." Reese pushed the paper back to him. "Good job, Brad."

He smiled. Brad looked at Reese. She was staring at him. She seemed to like what she saw.

He went back to his desk. Started working again. Reese returned to the front. She graded papers.

For some reason, factoring was easier now. The

answers didn't come quickly. But Brad followed Reese's steps. He could get to the answer. Eventually. He checked some answers with her.

Then the bell rang.

"Did you finish?" Reese asked.

"I just have five more problems. Thank you for helping me." Brad felt weird saying that. Still, he was glad Reese was the aide. He wouldn't want anyone else.

"When's your next match?" Reese organized Mr. Rey's papers.

"Tomorrow."

"Who are you playing?"

"Walnut."

Reese stared at him.

I should ask her to come to the game. How do I bring it up? Then he told himself not to think.

"You should come, if you want," he said.

"I'd love to see you play again." Reese was blushing.

"Okay." Brad smiled.

She's not just coming to watch tennis. She's coming to see me play.

Most of the students had left. Reese grabbed her backpack. Brad did the same.

"What's your next class?" she asked.

"Biology."

"I have English."

They walked out of class. Reese kept talking. So did Brad. Before he knew it, he had walked her to her English class.

CHAPTER 5

OVERHEAD

Brad didn't see Reese for the rest of the day. He was excited about what he'd learned. Reese was a great aide.

Tennis practice went well.

Brad couldn't believe it. His concentration was good. He was practicing with Julian.

Some of their rallies went long. Other players stopped practicing so they could watch.

"Dang! Just look at that. You guys are going for it," one player said.

Coach Kennedy liked to rotate players. After a few minutes, she matched Brad with Scott.

They eyed each other across the court.

"Okay, Brad." Scott smiled. He held up the ball to serve. "Get ready."

Brad knew Scott was referring to the last game. He was trying to make Brad remember how he'd blown it.

Whack!

The ball bounced a few feet away from Brad. He moved forward. Then hit it back.

Scott pivoted. He put the ball over the net. It bounced in front of Brad. He missed it.

"Oh man." Scott smirked. "Too bad. Too bad for you."

Eventually, it was Brad's serve.

"Come on, buddy," Scott teased. "Show me what you got!"

Brad served. Scott hit back. Brad hit it again. Scott quickly put it over the net.

Brad ran for it and missed.

"Dude!" Scott couldn't smile any wider. "You were so close. Too bad close doesn't matter. You blew it again."

Reese wasn't there. Thank goodness. Would she think Brad was a total loser?

Eventually a coaching assistant rotated the players.

The players changed opponents a few more times. Then practice was over.

"No wonder he's in *that* class," Scott said to a teammate. "He just doesn't get it."

Brad couldn't look at Scott. He knew he was talking about him. Brad wanted to say something. But he didn't.

Everyone went into the locker room. The players gathered around the assistant coach.

"Okay. Overall a very good practice," the assistant said. "We've posted the matches for the school scrimmage. They're on the door behind me. It's happening during lunch. You'll play one game, not a full set. So check those out. Then you're done."

The assistant moved out of the way. All of the players rushed toward the locker room door.

Brad couldn't see. But he could hear. Scott was laughing.

"Hey! They matched me against Brad," Scott said.

Brad stopped moving toward the door. He hung his head. Then he grabbed his tennis bag. Brad walked out of the locker room.

Julian stepped up beside him.

"Just ignore Scott," Julian said. "He's an idiot."

"Yeah."

Julian slapped his back. Then he turned and left.

Brad didn't know what to think. Scott was a jerk. He thought about Reese. He wondered if she knew Scott. Would she like Scott more?

He's so good at everything. He'd never blow a game. He'd never embarrass her. He's not in a resource class. He doesn't get confused like I do. What happens when she finds out I'm a loser?

He turned around. Walked back toward the

handball courts. Brad took out his tennis gear. He started hitting a ball against the wall. He started slow. Then he got faster. And faster.

His brain shut off. He didn't think about anything else.

CHAPTER 6

SMASH

Good game," Brad said. He shook his opponent's hand.

"Thanks." His opponent tried to smile.

They were playing the best out of five sets. Brad won the first three sets. The match was over.

Brad grinned as he left the court. He'd won the game in front of Reese.

"Some of my friends are going to the mall," Reese

said after the matches were over. "Do you want to go?"

"Together?" Brad was nervous. It was different than when he took a test. This felt good.

"Of course, Brad." Reese tried to sound exasperated. "I'll wait for you. Will you shower?"

"Sure. I'll be real quick." He grinned.

Reese smiled.

Brad quickly walked to the locker room.

"How can you not like Beyoncé?"

They were driving in her parents BMW. "Irreplaceable" was on the radio.

"I don't listen to a lot of music," Brad said.

"I love music."

"You ever listen to reggae?" he asked.

"Yeah, like Matisyahu?" Reese pressed a few buttons on the steering wheel. "You like this one?" It was the song "Warrior."

"Yeah. I like reggae because it's mellow."

"That's cool," Reese said. "I like being mellow."

"Do you watch a lot of movies?" Brad asked.

Normally, he didn't talk much. But Reese was easy to talk to.

"I love movies!" Reese was excited. "I loved all the *Harry Potter* movies. Have you seen *Divergent* or any of those films?"

"No. I like war movies." Brad looked at Reese. He hoped she wouldn't think he was weird.

"Really? That doesn't seem like you at all."

"It doesn't?" Brad tried not to overthink.

"You're so nice. Aren't those movies filled with blood and guts?"

"Sometimes." Brad took a breath. "I like the bravery."

Reese looked at Brad. He could tell she liked his answer.

The food court at the mall was packed. Kids from Valley were there. Some had been at the tournament. Others were just hanging out. The mall was *the* place to be.

Brad started to feel overwhelmed. *Breathe. Relax. Look people in the eye. Do all the things Mom and Dad tell me to do.*

"Great game," Shayla Roberts said. She was one of Reese's friends. She was standing with two more girls. Morgan and Thuy. They were Reese's friends too.

"Thanks." Brad smiled. "How's swimming?"

Shayla was one of Valley's top swimmers. Reese and Shayla were tight. They had apparently known each other since preschool.

"Good. Just trying to drop my times. I've got a meet tomorrow."

"Good luck."

Things only got better from there. Brad and Reese didn't talk a lot. But they stayed near each other. Brad talked with Morgan and Thuy. Why was today so much less awkward?

Brad also talked with Scott and Warren. Reese was at his side. That made him feel good.

"Good job, man." Scott high-fived him. As he did, Brad noticed him eyeing Reese.

"Thanks. You played well too." Brad was surprised. Scott was not his biggest fan.

"Yeah, he did. The other guy sucked." Warren laughed.

"I'm Scott." Scott extended his hand to Reese.

"Reese," she said. Reese shook Scott's hand.

"Man," Scott said. "You've got a strong grip."

"What can I say? I'm a strong girl."

Brad eyed Scott. He still held onto Reese's hand. She wiggled free.

"I have to talk to Morgan." Reese smiled at Brad. "BRB."

Brad nodded. He talked to Scott and Warren a few more minutes. Then they left. He was alone.

He saw some people from his resource class. They were too far away to talk to. Eventually, Reese walked back over. Her smile blew him away. He felt like the luckiest guy in the world.

"What are you doing Saturday?" Brad asked. They were driving home. The mall had been great. Brad was thrilled.

"I think I'm free in the afternoon. Do you want to hang out?" Reese gave him a reassuring smile.

"Sure," he said.

"It'll just be us this time. Think you can handle it?"

"Sure." Brad felt weird. Why wasn't he asking her out? He was the guy. But he had another date with Reese Caballero.

CHAPTER 7

DROP SHOT

Man, Brad had his mack on yesterday." Dominic smirked.

Brad didn't look up from his *Cuckoo's Nest* questions. They were a little harder today. What were his feelings about the book?

"What?" Kathryn asked.

"Yeah. You shoulda seen him," Edgar said. "He was with a fine white girl. That new one. Talking to her and all her friends."

Brad looked at them.

"You got a girlfriend, Brad?" Bernadette eyed him. She did that a lot. Brad ignored her.

"I'd date Brad." Kathryn smiled.

"You'd date Cohen." Dominic laughed.

"Shut up," Kathryn said.

"I don't hear working," Mr. Cohen called from his desk. He was typing on his computer. "I hear talking. Which means I also hear grades falling."

"You know what, Brad?" John asked. "You're like stupid hot."

"What do you mean?" Brad asked.

"Like, you're a good-looking dude. But you don't know it."

"And you're in this class," Dominic added.

Everybody cracked up.

Brad went back to his work. He didn't know if they were making fun of him or not. He did know Mr. Cohen would be coming over soon if they kept talking. He had work to finish.

"Why can't I be in an elective that period?" Brad

asked. He took a piece of bread from the basket.

Family night at Applebee's. He was with his parents. Brad liked Applebee's. Their hamburgers were tasty.

"Well," his dad said. "That class provides you with support."

"Yes, remember middle school?" his mom said. "Remember how long it took you to complete homework? This class works for you."

"And you can get help when you need it."

"But you guys help me," Brad said. "I just wish I could be somewhere else that period."

"Did something happen? You've never had a problem before with that class. You like Mr. Cohen, right?" His mom looked concerned.

Brad started to get nervous. He didn't want it to be a big deal. Being called "stupid hot" had bothered him. But he knew those students liked him. They just liked to joke around.

"No, I was just wondering." Brad took a sip of his lemonade.

"Aren't you in regular classes most of the day?" His dad took a bite of his bread.

"Yeah." Brad didn't like the term "regular classes."

He was confused. There was nothing wrong with being in a resource class. That's what his parents had always said. But now this? It made him feel different.

"I'm going to the movies with this girl on Saturday. Reese," Brad said.

His parents looked at him. Then they both smiled.

"You are?" his mom asked.

"Yeah, we met at the store last week. She saw me play tennis. The day I couldn't return that serve."

His parents asked him more questions. The whole time Brad felt good. Normal. He didn't want Reese to think he was different.

CHAPTER 8

SEED

Do you like Valley, Reese?" Brad's mom asked.

Reese had come to pick up Brad. It felt weird. Should he have gone to her house instead?

I need to get my license. I'm just so busy with school and tennis. I don't have time to study the driving handbook. God. I don't even have my permit yet!

"Yes. I really like the science department," Reese said. "I want to study molecular biology in college. I want to be a genetic engineer. I'm fascinated by DNA."

"Oh," Brad's parents said together. He could tell they were impressed.

I wish I were like that. I wish I were smart.

They were going to the movies. Brad had bought the tickets. They were going to see a John Green film.

"I love his books." Reese smiled as they walked into the theater. "Have you read any?"

"No." Brad smiled. "I saw one movie."

"Did you like it?"

"Yeah. But it was sad."

Brad bought popcorn and candy. Reese liked mixing the two. Brad was going to buy two sodas.

"Let's just share one," Reese said. "If I have a soda and candy, that's too much sugar."

Brad was glowing inside. Sharing a drink? That meant they had to use the same straw.

The theater wasn't full. They sat in the middle.

The lights dimmed. The previews started. Brad settled in.

He didn't normally watch movies like this. Chick flicks. He would've seen anything with Reese, though.

"Hey," Reese whispered in his ear.

Brad turned to look at her.

Then Reese kissed him. Her lips were soft. Softer than anything Brad had ever felt in his life.

They stared at each other. Then they kissed again. This was Brad's first kiss. And his second! He was glad it was with Reese.

"Hey, kids!" Scott called to them. He was standing on the patio of Periconi's Pizza. Brad often saw students there. It was the best pizza place. Nobody ever ate inside if they were cool.

The movie had gotten out thirty minutes before. Brad and Reese decided to walk around the mall.

"Hey," Brad said.

"Hi." Reese smiled. "Having some pizza?"

"Yeah." Scott picked up his plate. "This place is dope. There probably aren't places like this in Bay View."

"Oh, we have pizza," Reese said.

"Hey, Brad," Julian said. He was with Scott. "What are you up to?"

"We went to the movies."

"What'd you see?"

Brad had focus problems. He wanted to talk to Julian. But he didn't want to ignore Scott. Especially when Scott was talking to Reese.

"Hey, chill with us," Scott said to Reese.

Brad got nervous. *Would she leave me to hang out with them?*

"Nah. We've got other plans," Reese said. "But thanks."

"Okay. Later, man," Julian said. He shook Brad's hand.

"Later, Brad." Scott smiled. He shook his hand too.

Brad was surprised. Scott had never been nice to him. Not till he'd started hanging out with Reese.

Reese took Brad's arm in hers. They continued walking around the mall.

CHAPTER 9

BACKHAND

You should bring Reese on Saturday," Julian said.

Brad and Julian were walking to class on Monday. Brad was still on cloud nine.

Julian was having a party on Saturday. It was to celebrate the Valley High School tennis scrimmage. It would take place that Thursday at lunch.

"Okay, I'll ask her," Brad said.

"Cool. I'm so stoked for you. She seems really into you."

"Thanks."

"You should see if she can bring her friends. I'd like her to hook me up." Julian smiled. He patted Brad on the back as he walked into class.

Brad kept walking. He was taking Reese to a party. Wow! He was excited.

I'm a guy who gets invited to parties. She might like me more now.

He walked into the resource room.

People treat me like everyone else. She'll see.

Brad walked to tennis practice. He was feeling good. Most of his homework was done.

Reese had been helping him a lot in math. Today he had completed the assignment in class.

As Brad walked, he saw Reese across the campus. He admired how she moved. She was so confident. He didn't think he looked that way.

I always feel like I'm rushing.

He told himself to relax.

Then he saw Scott come out of the science

building. Reese walked toward Scott. He stood in front of her. Reese started to laugh.

Brad didn't know what Scott had said.

The two continued talking.

Brad got nervous. His body felt icy.

Does she like him? Why wouldn't she? He's better than me at everything. He's better at tennis. He's smarter. He's funnier than me too. She probably thinks he's better looking.

The two-minute bell rang.

Brad wanted to go over to them. He wanted to make sure his thoughts were just thoughts. He went to tennis practice instead.

"You feeling okay?" Julian asked.

They were rotating opponents.

Brad was not playing well. Julian kept scoring.

"Yeah," Brad said.

The serves kept coming. Brad tried to concentrate. Even when he was able to rally, Julian still scored.

"Come on, Brad," Coach Kennedy said. "Don't think. Just react."

Brad wanted to. He couldn't.

Another serve came fast and hard. Brad hit the ball. It smacked into the net.

"Darn it!" He squeezed his racket. Swatted the air.

"Maybe you should take a break," Coach Kennedy said.

"I'm fine," Brad snapped.

Coach Kennedy eyed him. Brad stared right back.

"Take a break, Brad."

Brad felt himself getting angry. He rarely got upset. It wasn't who he was. He didn't like people being mad at him.

"Fine." Brad moved off the court. He sat down on a bench.

He eyed Scott. Scott was on another court. Was he laughing at him? Brad was even more upset. He looked at the ground. Then closed his eyes.

CHAPTER 10

FOOT FAULT

Reese had just texted. Brad stared at it. He had just left practice. His tennis bag was slung over his shoulder.

REESE: What R U Up 2? Call l8r!

Why is she texting me? Hasn't she had enough of dating the stupid guy?

He imagined her telling Scott about math class. Brad figured they had shared a laugh. Man, was he stupid and slow. What had the resource guys said? Stupid hot. A sophomore in pre-algebra. And resource class? Forget about it.

He put his phone away. What could he text back? So he wasn't going to write anything.

"Well, I think we should put tile in," Brad's mom said.

They were sitting in the kitchen. It was dinnertime. Brad's mom had made meatloaf. It was a new recipe. Turkey was healthier than beef, she'd said.

Brad had only eaten a little. He was still thinking about Reese. Scott. Everything.

"If we're using carpet, then we should do wood floors," his dad said.

His parents were planning to remodel the house. Brad didn't understand anything about it.

He felt his phone buzz in his pocket. His parents didn't like technology at the table. He snuck a look.

Another text from Reese.

REESE: (R U still alive? :):)

Brad still hadn't replied.

He didn't want to be dumped. Reese was awesome. But so many things were in the way. It was out of control.

"It's Thursday. Right, Brad?" his dad asked. "Brad?"

Brad looked up. He slid his phone into his pocket.

"What?" Brad asked.

"Your scrimmage. At lunch?"

"Yeah."

"What time is lunch?" his dad asked.

"The bell rings at twelve fifteen."

"Are you going to see Reese this weekend?" his mom asked.

Brad remembered Julian's party. He'd been so excited. Now? Couldn't he turn back time? Things were better then.

CHAPTER 11

SIDELINE

Brad slept poorly. But he woke up feeling better.

I'm going to be more like Scott. I'm not going to let anything get to me.

As he walked to school, he continued to refine his plan.

Scott is always cool about everything. Nothing ever gets to him. If something gets to me? I'll think about what Scott would do.

He felt better the more he thought about it.

There was Reese. Brad took a deep breath. Then headed over to her.

Before he got there, Scott came out of nowhere. He tapped Reese on the shoulder. Then he moved so she couldn't see him. Reese laughed when she finally did.

He's always quicker than me.

Then Brad told himself not to think.

"Brad!" Reese smiled as he walked up. "I texted you yesterday. But didn't hear back."

"Yeah," Brad said.

He knew he needed a better answer. But Scott was still there.

"Why didn't you text her back?" Scott asked. He smiled slyly. "I'd never diss your text, Reese. That's just me. I have manners."

"It's no big deal," Reese said.

Brad didn't know what she meant. Was it really not a big deal?

"You'll have to forgive my friend here." Scott

put his arm around Brad. "He's in that special class."

Brad felt a jolt through his entire body. He wanted to slug Scott. What a nightmare. He shook his head. Then turned and walked away.

"Brad, come back!" Scott yelled.

No way was he going to let Scott pick on him again. Not in front of Reese.

CHAPTER 12

GRIP

Brad sat in Mr. Cohen's class. He was trying to work. It wasn't easy. He couldn't stop thinking about everything. He kept reading the same question over and over. Frustration was building.

"So, Brad," Dominic said. "Who you taking to the dance?"

Valley had dances all the time. One was in a couple of weeks. The theme was movies. Kids had to dress as their favorite character.

"I don't know," Brad said. He didn't look up from his paper.

"You don't know?" Edgar said. "You should take—"

"It's none of your business!" Brad yelled. He felt his body get rigid.

The room fell silent. Everybody looked at him. Brad eyed Mr. Cohen. Then he stood up and stormed out of class

Brad went over to a bench. There were a few people walking around.

He wanted to sit down. But he didn't. He didn't want to run into Reese. Nobody could see him like this. He never yelled. He never left class. Brad Kingsley was always respectful.

He took a deep breath. Tears pooled in his eyes. The feeling quickly went away.

He walked back toward class. Mr. Cohen was waiting outside for him.

"I'm sorry, Mr. Cohen," Brad said. He was

glad he didn't start crying. It had been a long time since he'd done that.

"Everything okay? Anything you want to talk about?" Mr. Cohen's spoke softly and slowly.

This was why Brad liked him. Brad didn't move fast. Except for tennis. Mr. Cohen talked like there was always time to work things out.

"I work hard in my classes," Brad said. "Most students don't try as hard. But they get it. I don't."

"You're different. They're different. That's all it is."

"I know."

"Sometimes you have to work harder."

"I *always* have to work harder, Mr. Cohen."

"But look at the results. You have great grades. You're a varsity tennis player." Mr. Cohen looked at Brad. "They may get some things more than you. You get some things they don't. And in some ways, they wish they were you."

Wanting to be him? No way. Still, his talk

with Mr. Cohen made him feel better. He got his stuff for the next class. Math.

Reese smiled at him when he walked in. He smiled as much as he could.

They had a test. Mr. Rey never gave homework on test days.

Thank God I don't need her help. I'm already so embarrassed.

It took him almost the whole period to take his test. He didn't look at Reese the entire time. He could feel her looking at him.

Once he was finished, he turned in the test. Then he went back to his desk and put his head down. The test went okay. But he felt like crap.

The rest of the day was shot. He skipped tennis practice. It was a first.

He just didn't care.

CHAPTER 13

SPIN

You were home before me today." Brad's mom put salad on the table. "That never happens," she said.

Brad was eating a piece of bread. He hadn't felt like eating all day. Now he was starving.

"Coach Kennedy let us out early. She doesn't want us to be too tired. Not before the tournament." Brad didn't like lying.

"Finished a project today at work," Brad's dad said. He put some lasagna on his plate. "I am so relieved."

Brad's dad worked with information systems. He talked tech a lot. Brad understood some of it. Most likely because he had been hearing about it his whole life.

"That's great, honey," his mom said. "But you know how it goes. You'll be knee-deep in something new tomorrow."

"What's wrong with me?" Brad blurted out.

Time stopped. His parents stared at him.

Brad had never really asked before. Whenever the subject came up, something happened. He got distracted. Nothing ever got resolved. Brad never got any answers.

"There is nothing wrong with you, Brad." His mom sounded sad. "It's just how your brain takes in information."

"You're a little different than some people," his dad said.

"But what if I don't want to be different? I have this thing I want to change. But I can't change it."

His parents stared at each other. They didn't

speak. Usually they had an answer for everything.

"You're fine just the way you are," his mom said. "I wouldn't want you to be any other way."

"Me neither," his dad said. "Just be you, Brad."

The next day at school, Reese confronted him. It was at the beginning of morning break.

Brad was trying to concentrate. He was avoiding her. But he wasn't fast enough.

"So, you're not talking to me?" Reese asked.

Brad looked into her eyes. They were cold now. All the warmth was gone.

He wanted to say "You're so perfect. Why do you care about me?" But he stayed silent.

"Say something, Brad."

He felt like she could read his mind.

"I've been busy."

"Really? That's your best excuse?" Her eyes narrowed.

Brad was getting super nervous. Reese was truly angry.

"I liked you a lot," she said. "I thought you liked me. I know you're in that resource class."

She let it sink in. Brad was speechless.

"I don't care about that. I don't judge people. You didn't even give me the chance to care. You made the choice for me."

Nobody had ever talked to him like this. He wanted to tell her how much he liked her. Brad wanted her to know he was worried about Scott. He was worried about the scrimmage. He was worried about the resource class.

But he just didn't feel like he could. It was so personal. He would be vulnerable. She would hurt him.

"Sorry," he said. Then he walked away.

"Okay," Coach Kennedy said to the team. "Everyone wears button-up shirts and ties tomorrow."

The tennis players groaned. They were standing on the court.

"I know it's just a school scrimmage. But

mindset is everything. I want you guys playing like it counts. You're representing our program. Your parents and peers are watching."

"Don't forget about the after-scrimmage party Saturday night!" Julian yelled.

Everybody cheered. Except Brad.

"And I'll be dancing with the hottest girl," Scott crowed. "Reese Caballero!"

Scott high-fived his friends.

Ouch! Brad's heart sank. He'd never felt so hurt.

Great. Now Scott's going to kick my butt in front of the whole school. And he also gets Reese.

Brad was angry. But not at Reese or Scott. He was angry at himself.

He had worried about the resource class. What would Reese think of him if she knew? And now his nightmare had come true.

I could take losing to anybody else. I just don't want to lose to that jerk. Maybe if I had asked her to the party. She told me she liked me!

But Brad knew the answer.

I just wasn't thinking fast enough. Didn't put it together. Too slow!

Brad often didn't get things. He didn't speak up. Didn't fight for what was right. He'd been okay with it before. But he wasn't okay with losing Reese.

CHAPTER 14

ACE

Brad didn't sleep well that night. He kept tossing and turning. The game with Scott was tomorrow. It haunted his dreams. He lost over and over to his rival.

Even worse? Brad couldn't talk to Reese.

He'd see her in a dream. She was right in front of him. He would open his mouth. But nothing came out.

He was over it. After throwing on his sweats, he went to school.

"You were almost here before me," a custodian said.

"Yeah," Brad said. "Sorry."

He was holding his tennis bag and backpack. Nobody was at the handball courts. He took out his racket and a ball.

He started hitting the ball back and forth. In no time he was doing it fast. Pretty soon he was sweating. He didn't think.

The ball. Keep your eyes on the ball. It's just you and the ball.

Brad started to think about everything. Reese. Scott. Resource class.

"The ball!" he yelled. "Hit the ball!"

His mind was clear again. He was focused. Ready for the day.

Nobody was in the locker room. Brad took a quick shower.

Then he dressed. He looked in the mirror to fix his tie.

"Looking sharp!" a basketball player said.

Brad smiled.

Despite everything, he felt better.

"Are you playing in the tennis game today?" Dominic asked.

They were sitting next to each other.

Edgar, John, Kathryn, and Bernadette were sitting at a table. Mr. Cohen was working with them.

Brad looked up from his *Cuckoo's Nest* questions. "Yeah." He only had four more to answer. The class had finished the work yesterday. His English teacher always gave him more time. Again, the questions were more personal. These always took Brad longer.

"You nervous?" Dominic asked

"Um ..." Brad didn't want to tell Dominic all. But he needed to talk. "Normally I wouldn't be. But I'm playing a guy who doesn't like me."

Brad wasn't going to tell him about Reese. It was too painful.

"He doesn't like you?" Dominic asked. "Why not?"

"Because I'm not as good as him."

"Really? This guy sounds like a punk."

"Well, I don't like calling people names. But he is a punk." Brad didn't like saying bad things about people. He almost never did. But maybe Scott deserved it just this once.

"Well, you have no choice. You have to beat him, right?"

"What do you mean?"

"You gotta play this fool," Dominic said. "No matter what, right?"

Brad nodded.

"You may as well beat him, right?" Dominic stared at Brad. "Who says you can't? You're on the team just like him."

They continued talking and working.

Brad realized something. Dominic was always

goofing around. He was always getting into trouble. That didn't mean he wasn't smart.

Brad saw Reese smiling as he walked onto the court.

Scott was already there. He was smiling too.

God. They're both laughing at me. Stop it! Just think about the game.

He did not want to be here. This was the toughest thing he had ever done. Why couldn't he be sick today? Scott would have thought he was faking it.

Fake it? Who cares? It would be better than this.

Brad saw his parents. They smiled at him.

Then he saw Mr. Cohen. He was sitting with Dominic, Edgar, John, Kathryn, and Bernadette. They were cheering and taking pictures with their phones.

Brad and Scott made eye contact. For whatever reason, Brad smiled.

Scott served first. Brad returned the serve. Scott hit the ball back.

You can do this! Watch the ball. You deserve to be here.

Brad swatted the ball back. Scott moved across the court. He lobbed it over the net.

Brad wasn't quick enough.

Scott scored. He needed to score three more times. They played until one of them got four points.

The ball was in play again. Back and forth. Back and forth.

Then Brad hit the ball into the net.

Scott looked smug. He spun his racket between his fingers.

Scott was up by two. He served again. It was short. Brad wasn't close enough. He couldn't make it to the ball. Scott scored another point.

Come on. One more point and it's over. Maybe I should give up. I can't score on the next three serves. That would be a tie. Then I'd have to get two more points. Nobody expects me to win.

Brad pulled himself away from the negative.

"Breathe," he said quietly. "Focus on the game. Focus on the ball."

Scott smiled as he served.

Brad raced across the court. Then he tipped the ball over the net.

Scott was too slow. He couldn't return it.

Brad scored.

The people watching clapped loudly.

Scott was still grinning. But Brad could tell the lost point bugged him.

The ball was in play. They each hit it back and forth.

Scott tried to lob it over the net. It didn't make it.

Brad scored another point.

Now Scott wasn't smiling. Brad didn't want to smile. But he couldn't help it. He was excited.

Come on. You got this!

And for the next few minutes, he didn't take his eyes off the ball.

Scott didn't score again for the rest of the match. He tried. But Brad was in control. He had answers for everything. He was focused. Like he had been on the handball court.

The match ended. Brad had won. He was elated. It was a great win.

"That was dope, Brad," Dominic said. He shook his hand.

"You smoked him." John smiled.

"You're so good! Will you teach me?" Kathryn gave him a hug.

"Teach us," Bernadette said. She took Brad's tennis racket. She examined the strings.

"Sure." Brad smiled as she gave him back his racket.

They walked away. Brad's parents came up.

"You were amazing!" his mom said.

"You were so calm out there." His dad patted him on the shoulder.

Brad looked over at Scott. He was still standing on the court. Confusion was written on his face.

"He never thought I could beat him," Brad said.

"You didn't just beat him." His dad lowered his voice. "You kicked his butt!"

Brad looked around for Reese but didn't see her.

CHAPTER 15

GRAND SLAM

Brad didn't see Reese for the rest of the day. She wasn't in math class that Friday either.

After yet another math test, Brad asked where she was.

"Admin needed her somewhere else." Mr. Rey sighed. "Don't worry, Brad. I can help you until we get some support."

"Oh," Brad said. "Is there any chance she might come back?"

"Maybe. Reese is an office aide. They can put her wherever they need her."

Brad felt awful.

I was such a jerk to her.

The bell rang. The students got up and left.

Brad just sat there. He hoped there was a chance Reese would come back.

Deep down, he knew she wouldn't.

She probably doesn't want to be around me ever again.

"She's going to be there with Scott," Brad said. "Why should I go to Julian's party?"

He was talking to his parents. They were in the living room. His parents were watching a recorded TV program.

"Because you were invited," his dad shot back. "If you don't show up? People will stop asking, Brad."

"I go to things."

"When?" his mom asked. "You keep talking

about being 'normal.' You want to do what everybody else does. Well, this is what people your age do. They go to parties with their friends."

Brad thought about it. He wanted to tell them he was scared. He didn't want to see Reese with Scott. But he couldn't. He knew his mom was right.

"Okay. I'm going to change my clothes."

Brad walked to Julian's. The night air was cool. As he got closer, he started to feel nervous. Soon he was overwhelmed.

There were people everywhere. They were inside. They were on the front lawn. They were in the driveway. Some people were standing in the street. They were chatting together. Texting. Talking on their phones. Eating. It was crazy.

Turn around. Just walk around the neighborhood. Mom and Dad will never know I didn't go.

He kept moving forward.

Julian invited me. I have every reason to be here.

It was just like being on the varsity team. It

was just like everything else. Brad could do everything just like everybody else. He just might do it differently.

"What's up, Brad?" Julian gave him a handshake and bro hug.

"Not much," he said.

A few of the other people on the tennis team said hello.

"Have some food," Julian said. "We have a ton of sodas and pizza."

"Thanks. Sounds good."

Julian patted Brad on the back. Then he walked off.

Brad moved into the house. He wasn't very hungry.

Scott was dancing. But not with Reese. Where was she?

A few students stopped him. They told him how great the tennis game had been.

Brad walked over to the food. More people said hi. He found a Dr. Pepper.

Where was Reese? He couldn't find her.

The music was loud. The house was crammed. But Brad started to relax. He opened the soda and took a drink.

Brad talked to people for an hour. He felt good. Maybe he could go home now. He started to look for Julian. He was going to say goodbye.

That was when he ran into Reese. She had just shown up. Her friends were behind her. Wow! Brad thought she looked beautiful.

"You're here," Reese said. She was surprised. She knew he didn't like crowds.

Any second now he expected Scott to come over. He'd probably smile. Then he'd put his arm around her. They might even kiss.

No way did he want to see that. But he didn't want to leave. Not now.

"Yeah," Brad said. "I was just going."

"I'm glad I got to see you." Reese smiled. The same smile as always. She didn't seem mad at him. It made him feel better.

"Scott's here," Brad said. He didn't know what else to say.

"So what?" Her expression hardened. "I'm not with him. He thought I was coming with him. The only thing I told him was that I might dance with him. One time."

"Oh."

"But I also might be too busy." Reese smiled at him again.

It was clear. Brad got it. He understood.

"You've been so weird about everything," Reese said. "Brad, you know I like you. I thought you liked me—"

"I do like you. I like you a lot. I think you're beautiful."

Reese grabbed him. She gave him a hug. Brad hugged her back.

She felt good against him. Strong. Supportive.

"I'm sorry," he whispered in her ear. "Sometimes it's hard for me to think. Do the right thing. I get stuck."

"That happens to me too." Reese looked at him. She was still smiling. "You're not alone, Brad."

Brad stayed at the party. He almost never left Reese's side.

He talked with Julian and a few other tennis players. Everyone was excited about the season.

Brad looked around the room. Nobody was looking at him. Nobody was judging him. His fears fell away.

Then he saw Scott. He was dancing with yet another girl. Scott looked at him. Gave him a nod. Even smiled.

Brad nodded. His arm found Reese. He brought her to his side. She was all he was going to think about now.

The weekend was over. It was Monday. Brad and Reese were walking to class.

"Let's do something after practice today," Brad said.

"I have to study for a test." Reese frowned.

"Oh."

"Tomorrow?" Reese asked.

"Sure." Brad smiled.

They walked past Brad's resource class. Reese's class was a few doors down.

They walked up to her classroom.

"Well, see you at the break." Reese squeezed his hand.

"Yeah. I'll meet you at the bench. The one outside this building."

"Great." She leaned in. Then she gave him a quick kiss. It was just a peck, but it completely stunned him. High school had never been better.

"Bye." Reese went into her class.

Still in a daze, Brad walked into the resource room. He put his backpack on his desk.

Dominic was there. He wore his earbuds.

Brad saw Mr. Cohen across the room. He was helping some students already.

Brad felt himself getting nervous. He had

questions about his math assignment from last week. Mr. Rey hadn't found an aide. Reese was working in a special education class that period.

"I love it! Those students are awesome," she had said. "But I do miss working with you."

He took out his math book and sat down. Ten problems to go. If he didn't get help, he'd be swamped. These problems plus more homework? Disaster.

His breathing got shallow. He tried to focus on the next problem. But he just stared at the numbers, confused.

Relax. You will be fine.

He took a deep breath. And another one. And another.

He started working through the problems.

And before he knew it, he was okay.

WANT TO KEEP READING?

9781680211092

Turn the page for a sneak
peek at another book in the
White Lightning series:

REBEL

CHAPTER 1

TO SEE THE WORLD

Dear Patrick,

Thank you for your letter. Your family and home in America sound very nice. I would like to visit your country one day. I would especially like to see Disneyland. And I would like to meet Mickey Mouse.

You asked me to describe my home and myself. I live in a small village in Africa. It is the dry season now. It is very dusty. In a few months the rains will come. Then the

1

ground will turn muddy. The grass will grow. I don't like mud. But we need the grass for our cattle.

I have a mother and father. I also have three younger sisters. I have many aunts, uncles, and cousins. Two of my grandparents live in our village. Our house is round. Our roof is made of reeds. The school is square. It has a blue metal roof. It is loud when the rain falls.

My best friend is Jojo. We play soccer. Only we call it football. Do you like football? I like it. I would play it all day long if I could. But I like school too. I like learning about the world. My favorite subject is geography. I want to become a teacher one day.

I am looking forward to being your pen pal.

Sincerely,
Koji

I set my pencil down. Most of my classmates are still writing. Including Jojo. Maybe I should write more. But I read over my letter. Decide it's enough. I hope Patrick writes back. I want to learn more about his life halfway around the world. I pick up my pencil again. Write a note at the bottom of the page.

Please tell me more about your life in America.

There. Now it's enough.

"Time to finish," Mr. Wek says.

Pencils hit the desks.

"Put your letters in the envelopes you addressed," he says. "Pass them to me. I will see that they get mailed."

I watch my letter. It goes hand over hand to the front of the classroom. The beginning of its long journey. I wonder how it will travel. By plane? By boat? I wish I could travel with it.

"Get out your math books," Mr. Wek says.

A few students groan. Jojo too. They don't like math. I don't mind it. I'm going to be a teacher. So I will need to know many things.

It's the end of the day. I'm restless. Want to go outside. But I try to sit still. Don't want a scolding from Mr. Wek. Finally he says, "History exam tomorrow. You may go."

Jojo and I are the first out of our seats. "Race you home," he says.

The village is a mile north. We run the whole way. I sprint at the end. But he still beats me.

"Hah! I won!" he shouts. He throws his hands in the air. Like he's a big champion.

"I'll beat you one of these days," I tell him.

"No you won't," he says. "My legs will always be longer than yours."

"Maybe. But I'm a better footballer."

He laughs. "You are not."

"Am so." I run to our hut. Grab my football. But I don't leave quickly enough.

"Koji!" my mother says. "Change out of your

uniform. And put down that ball. I need you to fetch water."

I groan. "Why can't Onaya do it?"

"Because she's helping me cook. Go on."

I quickly change out of my yellow uniform. I grab the plastic water jug. Carry it outside.

Jojo is playing football with his brothers. I sneak up behind him. Steal the ball out from under his foot. "Hey!" he shouts.

"See?" I laugh. "I told you I'm better!"

I play with them for a few minutes. I'm still holding the water jug. I'm tempted to set it down. And really play. But I need to get going or Mama will be angry.

The pump is at the other end of the village. I pass the village leader's hut. He sits outside. A number of men sit around him. My father's there. I'm surprised to see Papa here. He's usually out with our cattle.

I leave the path. Step closer to them. One man points south. Another points west. They speak in hushed and hurried voices. The one word I hear sends a chill through me. "Soldiers."

Papa spies me. Shoos me away.